Chuntao

Author: Dishan Xu
Translator: Ying Hua

CHICAGO ACADEMIC PRESS

Chuntao
Author: Dishan Xu
Translator: Ying Hua
Language: English
Publisher: Chicago Academic Press
Word Count (for space of all pages): 25000 words
Publishing Date: December 30, 2024
ISBN 978-1-965890-06-6

Publishing   Chicago Academic Press
              Chicago Illinois
E-mail   contact@chicagoacademicpress.com
Website   http://chicagoacademicpress.com/

Book Size   5X8 inches
First Edition December 30, 2024

About the Translator

Ying Hua is an associate professor at School of Foreign Languages, Shanghai Dianji University. She holds a doctorate in applied linguistics from the Hong Kong Polytechnic University. She was awarded International Visiting Scholar Fellowship by China Scholarship Council (CSC) in 2024. She published a monograph *The Construction of Corporate Identities by Chinese and American Airlines on Social Media: A Cross-Cultural Multimodal Study* with Springer and 7 articles indexed in key academic journals.

This summer was exceptionally hot. Although the street lights were bright, the vendor selling sour plum soup at the alley entrance was still performing with his copper bowl, much like a girl performing the "Pear Blossom Drum", a traditional Chinese folk art that includes singing and drumming. A woman carrying a large basket of waste paper with written characters walked past him. Although her face couldn't be seen clearly under her tattered straw hat, when she greeted the vendor, it was apparent she had a full set of snow-white teeth. She bore such a heavy load on her back that she could not stand straight but paced solemnly, step by step, like a camel, to her own door.

There was a small courtyard inside. The woman lived in two remaining rooms of a collapsed wing. A large part of the yard was covered with rubble. In front of her door, she had planted a trellis of cucumbers and several rows of corn. Under the window, there were a dozen evening primrose plants. A few decayed beams lay across the bottom of the trellis, which constituted probably the most valuable seating in her home. As she approached her door, a man came out of the room and hurried to help her unload her heavy burden.

"Honey, you're back late today."

The woman looked at him, seemingly surprised by his words. "What do you mean? Are you crazy about a wife? Don't call me 'honey', I say." As she stepped inside, she took off her tattered straw hat and casually hung it on the back of the door, then grabbed a small bamboo scoop from the side of the tank to repeatedly draw water from it, drinking until she couldn't breathe anymore. After opening her mouth for a while, she went under the melon shed, dragged the basket to the side and sat down on the decayed beam.

The man was named Liu Xianggao. The woman was about the same age as him, in her thirties, and her maiden name was also Liu. Apart from Xianggao, no one knew her name Chuntao. The neighbors called her Aunt Liu who collected waste paper because she worked in the garbage dumps on the streets and alleys all day long, sometimes yelling, "Waste paper for lanterns". She worked in the hot sun and cold wind all day long, but she was born with a love of cleanliness. No matter the season, she had to wash up and clean her face every day upon returning home. The one who prepared the water for her usually was Xianggao.

Xianggao was a graduate of a rural primary school. Four years ago, during a war in his village, his family was scattered. On the road, he met Chuntao, who was also fleeing, and they walked together for hundreds of miles before they were separated again.

She followed other refugees to Beijing. As a western woman in the Zongbu Hutong wanted to hire a countryside girl without past experience as a "nanny", she was recommended for the job. The woman saw that Chuntao was beautiful and liked her very much. She noticed that her master always ate beef, spread butter on the steamed buns, and added milk to her tea, which created a strong, unpleasant smell that she couldn't get used to. One day, the master asked her to take the child to Sanbeizi Garden. She felt that the smell of the master's house was somewhat similar to that coming from a den of tigers and wolves, which made her feel increasingly uncomfortable. Hence, she resigned in less than two months. Given that in ordinary households as a rural person she was not used to being a servant and couldn't stand being scolded, she quit her job again soon. At her lowest point, she chose to collect waste paper in exchange for a living, whereby she could barely make ends meet for a day.

Xianggao had a quite simple experience after parting with Chuntao. He went to Zhuozhou but couldn't find any relatives. There were a couple of friends of the family who were reluctant to let him stay, upon hearing that he had fled as a refugee. He had no choice but to come back to Beijing. Through others' introduction, he met Mr. Wu, who sold sour plum soup at the entrance of the hutong. Mr. Wu lent him the shabby courtyard where he was living now, but he mentioned that if someone came to rent it, he would have to find another place. He had nothing to do but helped Mr. Wu work out accounts and sell goods. He got free housing and food, earning just enough for two meals a day. Chuntao's paper-collecting business gradually improved. However, not allowed to pile up her goods where she had lived, she searched for a new place to live along the walls of Deshengmen. One day, when she knocked at a door, it was Xianggao, her acquaintance. Without going through many procedures, she rented the house from Mr. Wu and invited Xianggao to stay with her to help her out. This was what had happened three years ago. He could recognize a few characters and would pick out some items that could sell for a decent price from the written papers that Chuntao found and exchanged, like pictures or couplets and letters written by certain generals or high-ranking officials. Their collaboration led to greater progress in their business. Xianggao sometimes taught her to recognize some characters, but it was not very effective, as he himself didn't know many, and understanding characters was even harder.

In the years they lived together, their life together could be likened not so much to that of mandarin ducks, but rather to that of a pair of sparrows.

Let's get back to the main story. When Chuntao entered the house, Xianggao was already following her with a bucket of water in his hand. He said in a cheerful tone, "Honey, come on, wash up. I'm getting hungry. Let's have something nice to eat tonight—scallion pancakes, what do you think? If you agree, I'll go and buy some scallions and sauce."

"Honey, honey, don't call me like that, all right?" Chuntao said impatiently.

"Just promise me this and tomorrow I'll buy you a nice hat at the Tianqiao market. Didn't you say it's time for a new hat?" Xianggao pressed his request.

"I wouldn't like to hear it."

He realized that she was a bit displeased, so he changed to ask, "What's for dinner? Just tell me!"

"You can eat whatever you want. Just go and buy it."

Xianggao returned with some scallions and a bowl of sesame paste, placing them on the table in the main room. After taking a bath, Chuntao came out holding a red letter.

"Which prince's wedding letter is this? She asked. "Don't give it to Mr. Li on the market again this time. If we have someone take it to Peking Hotel, we can sell it for a better price."

"That's ours. Otherwise, how could you be my wife? After teaching you a couple of characters for a year or two, you even can't recognize your own name!"

"Who can recognize all these characters? Stop calling me 'honey'—I don't like it. Who wrote this?"

"I filled it out. When the police came to check the household registration this morning, they said there would be a stricter curfew these days and every household had to report accurately how many people lived there. Mr. Wu advised us to write as if we were a couple to avoid troubles. The police also said that it was inappropriate to write 'cohabitants' for a man and a woman. So I filled in the blank letter we didn't sell last time. I wrote down that we got married in the Lunar Year of Xinwei.”

“What? Year of Xinwei? How can I recognize you then? Don’t mess around! We’ve never held a wedding ceremony, nor had a cross-cup wine ceremony, so we’re not a couple.”

Chuntao said this somewhat reluctantly but still spoke calmly. She changed into a pair of blue cloth trousers, white on top. Though she had no makeup on, her natural beauty shone through. If she was willing to get married, according to the matchmaker a woman like her at around twenty-three or twenty-four years old could reasonably be worth at least one hundred eighty.

She smiled, rolling that letter into a long

strip, saying, "Stop messing around with the wedding letter! Just eat the pancakes." She lifted the stove lid and threw the strip into the fire, then went to the table to knead the dough.

Xianggao said, "Let it burn. After all, the police have already registered us as a couple. If the government looks into the wedding letter, can't I say I lost it while fleeing. From today on, I'm going to call you my wife. Mr. Wu acknowledges it. The police acknowledge it. I'm still going to call you that even if you don't expect. Honey! Honey! Tomorrow I'll buy you a hat. I can't afford a ring."

"If you keep calling me that, I'm going angry."

"It seems you're still thinking about Li

Mao." Xianggao said, no longer cheerful as before. He said it himself, and he didn't necessarily want Chuntao to hear it, but she did.

"I miss him? We've been a married couple for one night, but we haven't heard from each other for four or five years. Missing is a waste of time, isn't it?" Chuntao said. She had once told Xianggao about the situation on the day she got married. The bridal sedan had entered the door. Before the guests were seated, someone from the other two villages in front came to notify that a large group of soldiers had arrived, rounding up people to dig trenches, which scared everyone into fleeing. The newlyweds quickly packed their things and followed the crowd to escape westward. They walked together for a day and a night. On the second night, there were shouts ahead, "The bandits are coming. Get out of here!" At that time, only concerned about hiding, no one can look after anyone else. Until dawn, more than a dozen people had been missing, including her husband Li Mao. She continued with her earlier words, "I think he must have gone with the bandits, and maybe he was killed early on. Alright, let's not talk about him."

She finished cooking the pancakes and brought them to the table. Xianggao ladled a bowl of cucumber soup from the casserole, and everyone kept silent as they ate. After finishing the meal, they sat under the melon shed to chat as usual. Tiny stars twinkled among the melon leaves. The cool breeze brought fireflies to the shed as if stars were falling down. The evening jasmine gradually emitted its fragrance, suppressing the surrounding stench. "The tuberose smells so good!" Xianggao picked a flower and tucked it into Chuntao's hair. "Don't spoil my tuberose. I'm not a brothel girl who wears flowers at night." She took it off, smelled it, and then placed it on a decayed beam above her. "Why did you come back so late today?" Xianggao asked.

"Oh! I made a great deal today! This afternoon, just as I was about to go home, I passed by the back door and saw a cleaner pushing a cart full of waste paper. I asked him where he got it. He said it was discarded out of Shenwu Gate. I saw piles of red and yellow inside and asked if he was selling it. He allowed me to take it at a bit lower price. Look!" She pointed at the large basket below the window, "I spent a dollar and bought this whole large basket! Whether I made a profit or not, who knows? I'll check it out tomorrow."

"Goods from the palace are never wrong. I'm just afraid of goods that come from schools or foreign trade firms. They are heavy, smell bad, and it's hard to tell if they are worth anything."

"In recent years, people on the streets are increasingly using foreign newspapers for wrapping things. I don't know where so many people interested in foreign newspapers come from. When you pick them up, they are really heavy, but you can't sell them for much."

"The more people read foreign books, the more people want to read foreign newspapers, hoping to be involved in foreign business in the future."

"While they're getting into foreign business, we're just collecting paper with foreign words."

"In future, I'm afraid that everything will have foreign labels. Pulling a cart means pulling a foreign cart. Driving donkeys means driving foreign donkeys. Maybe there will even be foreign camels coming." Xianggao made Chuntao laugh.

"You shouldn't talk about others first. If you had money, you would also like to read foreign books and marry a foreign wife."

"God knows I will never get rich. Even if I get rich, I won't marry a foreign woman. If

I had money, I would go back to the countryside and buy a few acres of land for us to farm together."

Ever since Chuntao fled, she lost her husband. When she heard the word "countryside", she never felt good about it. She said, "You still want to go back? I'm afraid we'll have lost money and family before buying a field. I won't go back even if I cannot afford living."

"I mean going back to our countryside in Jin County."

"In this age, every countryside is the same. If there's no war, there will be thieves; if there are no thieves, there will be Japanese invasion. Who dares to go back? It's better to collect waste paper here. What we're short of now is just a helping hand. If there were someone at home to help you sort things out, you could have gone out to set up a stall during the day in order to avoid losing sales when commodities are passed through others' hands."

"I still have to learn for three more years before I can manage. Losing sales is not attributed to others but my shortage of insight. I've learned quite a lot over these past few months. In terms of stamps, I can almost tell which ones are valuable and which aren't. In terms of letters by notable figures, I have some confidence in telling which ones can sell well and which ones can't. A few days ago, I found a piece of calligraphy by Kang Youwei among that pile of written paper. How much do you think I sold it today?" He gladly held out his thumb and forefinger to show, "Eighty cents!"

"That's true! It will be pretty good if you can find eighty cents a day in this pile of waste paper. Why go back home to farm? Isn't that just asking for trouble?" Chuntao's cheerful voice sounded like the singing of orioles in the deep spring. She continued, "I can guarantee that there are some good finds in this pile for you. I have heard that there will be even more tomorrow. That person told me to wait for him at the back door early in the morning. People in the palace are busy packing up and sending things south these days, and there are a lot of unwanted waste paper in the warehouse. I saw plenty of them outside Donghua Gate, being thrown out bag after bag. You should ask around tomorrow, too."

After talking a lot, they didn't realize that it had already been past the second watch. She stretched and stood up, saying, "I'm tired today. Let's have a rest!"

Xianggao followed her into the room. Under the window was tukang (a type of traditional heated earth bed) wide enough for two or three people to sleep on. In the dim light, a humorous painting of Eight Immortals playing mahjong on one side of the wall and a cigarette company's advertisement featuring the slogan "He's Still the Best" on the other side were faintly visible. Chuntao would look stylish as the modern women in that advertisement if she removed her tattered hat, found an outdated cheongsam to wear by rummaging through footbridges, not to mention Ruifuxiang or other Shanghai garment stores, and sat in any grass field. Therefore, Xianggao often joked that the photo on the wall was actually a small portrait of Chuntao.

She climbed onto the bed, took off her clothes, casually pulled a quilt to cover herself, and lied down on one side. Xianggao gently pressed her back and kneaded her legs as usual. Her daily fatigue was thus alleviated with a little smile in the flickering light of the small oil lamp. In a half-sleepy state, she murmured, "Brother Xiang, you should also go to sleep. Don't work late. We have to get up early tomorrow." When the woman gradually began to emit faint snores, Xianggao extinguished the lamp.

As soon as dawn broke, the two flew out

of the nest like crows searching for food, each busy with their own business. Just following the noon cannon shot, the sound of gongs and drums at Shishahai has gone overwhelming. Chuntao came out from the back door, carrying a paper basket and heading toward the west side, near the bridge. At the intersection of the temporary market, she suddenly heard someone calling out to her, "Chuntao, Chuntao!" Even Xianggao seldomly called her by her nickname throughout a year. Since she left the countryside, no one had called her that for four or five years.

"Chuntao, Chuntao, don't you recognize me anymore?"

She couldn't help turning her head to take a look, only to see a beggar sitting by the road. That pleading voice came from his bearded mouth. He could not stand up because both his legs were broken. He wore a gray tattered military uniform whose white iron buttons were all rusty. His shoulders were exposed through the torn epaulettes and a tattered military cap was tilted on his head with its badge long gone. Chuntao stared at him, speechless.

"Chuntao, it's me, Li Mao!"

She took two steps forward. Tears mixed with dust had penetrated into the messy beard of the man.

Her heart was beating heavily and she couldn't speak for a long time, but finally said, "Brother Mao, you are a beggar here? How did you lose your legs?"

"Ah, it's a long story. How long have you been here? What are you selling?"

"What am I selling! I'm collecting waste paper. Let's have more talk when we get back home."

She rent a rickshaw, helped Li Mao up, placed her basket on the vehicle, and pushed it from behind. When they went all the way to the foot of Desheng Gate, the rickshaw driver helped her assist Li Mao down. As they entered the alley, while knocking on a small copper bowl, Mr. Wu asked, "Aunt Liu, you're back home early today. How's business today?"

"Here comes a countryman." She

responded.

Li Mao crawled like a little bear cub, with both hands pressed against the ground, helping his two broken legs crawl.

She took out a key from her pocket, opened the door, and led the man inside. She took out a set of Xianggao's clothes. Then she went to the well, fetched two buckets of water, and poured it into a small tub to teach the man how to wash himself just as Xianggao did every day. Afterwards, she poured another basin of water for him to wash his face. Then she helped him sit on the bed and washed herself in the open air.

"Chuntao, your room is very tidy. Do you live here by yourself?"

"There's another fellow." Chuntao answered him without hesitation.

"Have you started a business?"

"Haven't I told you it's just collecting waste paper?"

"Collecting waste paper? How much can you make in a day?"

"Don't interrogate me first. Please tell me your story first."

Chuntao poured out the water, came back into the room tidying her hair, and sat down opposite Li Mao. Li Mao began to tell his story,

"Chuntao, alas, there is a lot to say! Let me summarize.

Ever since that night when I was captured by the bandits, I hated them as I couldn't see you. Having seized a rifle from them, I shot two of them dead and escaped desperately. I fled to Shenyang. As it happened that the border army was recruiting soldiers, I enlisted. During the three years in the military camp, I was always asking for news from home. It was said that our village had turned into a brick-and-tile land. We don't even know whose hands our land deed is in now. When we escaped, we forgot to take the land deed with us. Hence, during these past few years, I haven't asked for a leave to go back home. If I had asked for a leave, I was afraid that I might have lost only a few yuan's military pay.

I kept a low profile in the army, hoping for my monthly pay, and didn't dare to expect a promotion. But it seems this was my destiny: At the beginning of last year, the regiment commander suddenly issued an order saying that if any soldier in the regiment could hit the target nine times consecutively, he would receive double pay and a promotion. No one in the entire regiment hit the target even four times consecutively. Even if the target was hit, the hit was still not in the bullseye. However, I hit the target nine times consecutively in the bullseye and never missed the last bullet. Back turned, waist bent, and head facing the ground, I tried to show off my skills. I shot the gun from between my legs, perfectly hitting the bullseye without any deviation. How joyful I was at that moment!

The regiment commander had someone bring me to him. I was thinking to myself that I would at least hear a few words of praise. But to my surprise, that bastard turned hostile, suddenly accused me of being a bandit and wanted to shoot me. He said if I weren't a bandit, my marksmanship wouldn't be so accurate. My section commander and squad leader pleaded for me, vouching that I wasn't a bad person. I managed to escape being executed, but he stripped me of my proper soldier rank and wouldn't allow me to be a substitute soldier either. He said that as an officer, it was inevitable to offend his soldiers. If he supervised the combat on the front line and there was someone like me who aimed so accurately and shot from behind, it's not worth dying at the hands of an enemy although counted as being killed in action as well. All had nothing to say and just advised me to leave the army and find another way to make a living.

Soon after I was discharged, the Japanese occupied Shenyang. I heard that bastard commander led his army to make a surrender first. At this, I couldn't hold back my anger and thought of ways to go find that traitor. I joined the volunteer army and fought near Haicheng for several months, retreating into the pass while fighting. Last month in the northeast of Pinggu, while I was on watch, I encountered the enemy and got both legs injured. At that time, I could still walk, so I hid under a large rock and shot a few of them dead. I couldn't hold on any longer, so I threw away my gun and crawled towards the pathway along the field. I waited for one day, two days, and still no one from the Red Cross or the Red Crescent came. The wound went more and more swollen. I was unable to walk and had no food or water, only to lie on one side, waiting to die. Later, a large vehicle happened to pass by and the driver helped me up and took me to the tent of a military doctor. They didn't even examine me and just threw me onto a truck which transported me to a field hospital. I had already been injured for three days. When the doctor opened the bandages, he said that the wounds were all rotten and had to be amputated. I stayed in the hospital for more than a month. Luckily, I recovered, but lost both of my legs. Given that I had no relatives around here and couldn't go back to the countryside; even if I would go back, how could I farm without legs, I begged the hospital to take me in and give me some work to do. But the doctor said the hospital only took care of curing me rather than keeping me or finding work for me. There was no veteran's home for disabled soldiers here, which forced me to go out for begging. Today is just the third day. I have often thought these two days that if this continues, I won't be able to bear it anymore and have to hang myself."

Chuntao listened attentively to him and she didn't know when her eyes became moist. But she remained silent. Li Mao wiped the sweat from his forehead with his hand and took a break for a while.

"Chuntao, how have you been in the past few years? Though this small place may not be as spacious as ours in the countryside, it seems that you haven't suffered a lot."

"Who hasn't suffered? No matter how tough it is, we still have to find a way to live. Can't a smiling face be seen in front of Yama? For the past few years, I've been living by collecting waste paper to trade for lamp oil, and I have a partner named Liu. We can say that we two are inseparable, barely managing to get by."

"Are that man named Liu and you co-habiting in this room?"

"Yes, we sleep on this bed together." Chuntao did not hesitate at all. It seemed that she had long had such a preconceived notion.

"So, you have been married to him?"

"No, we're just living together."

"Then do you still consider yourself my wife?"

"No, I'm not anyone's wife."

Li Mao's sense of husbandhood was provoked. He couldn't think of what to say. He stared at the ground not for any particular reason but because he just felt a bit shy about looking at his wife. Eventually, he murmured, "If this goes on, people will laugh at me, calling me a live turtle."

"Turtle?" The woman reacted to his words, a bit annoyed, but she kept calm. She continued, "Only the rich and powerful fear being called a turtle. As for you, who recognizes you, living without a name and dying without a surname? What does it matter whether you're a turtle or not? Right now, I am myself. Whatever I do will not tarnish your name."

"We are still a couple after all. There goes an old saying, 'A night of marriage brings a hundred days of affection.'"

"I don't know whether there is really a hundred days of affection between us." Chuntao interrupted him, "As for a hundred days, it's been over a dozen of the hundred days. In these four or five years, we haven't known each other's whereabouts. I assume that you haven't expect to run into me here. I'm all alone here, and I need to survive, needing help from others. Given that we've lived together all these years, in terms of affection mine for you is naturally much weaker. I brought you back today because my father had a friendship with yours and we were fellow folks. If you choose to recognize me as your wife, I do not acknowledge you as such. Even if we go to court, you may not necessarily win."

Li Mao fumbled with his belt, as if he wanted to take something out, but his hand suddenly stopped. He glanced at Chuntao and eventually withdrew his hand, resting it on the mat.

Li Mao said nothing, and Chuntao cried. The sun shadow quietly shifted for three or four minutes during this time.

"All right, Chuntao, it depends on you. You see, I'm already a cripple. Even if you're willing to live with me, I'm not capable of sustaining you." Li Mao finally made these wise utterances.

"I can't abandon you just because you are disabled, but I feel reluctant to part with him. We all live together, and no one needs thinking of sustaining someone else, OK?" Chuntao also conveyed her true feelings.

Li Mao's stomach made a faint rumbling sound.

"Oh, after talking for so long, I haven't even asked what you want to eat! You must be very hungry."

"Everything is fine. I'll eat whatever you have. I haven't eaten since last night and just drank some water."

"I'll go buy something." Chuntao was just stepping out of the door when Xianggao walked in happily from the courtyard. They bumped into each other under the melon trellis. "Why are you so happy? Why are you back so early today?"

"Today I made a great deal! When in the morning I opened the basket you carried back yesterday, I found a package of official documents by the King of Goryeo during the Ming Dynasty. Each can sell for at least fifty yuan. Now we have ten at hand! I just gave a few to the dealer to see how much masters could offer, and then I'll distribute the rest. There are also two sheets of paper stamped by the Imperial Seal of the Duanming Palace. An expert said they were from the Song royal family and offered me a quote of sixty yuan. I didn't dare to sell them, afraid that I might miss a better deal. So I brought them back to show you. Look~" While talking, he opened the old blue cloth bundle in his hand and took out the official documents and old sheets of paper. "This is the Imperial Seal of the Duanming Palace." He pointed at the imprint on the paper.

"Without this imprint, I couldn't have found any benefits. The foreign promotional sheet is even whiter than this. Why don't the officials in charge understand it just like me? Although Chuntao looked at it, she didn't understand what the value of that paper was.

"Understand what the value is? If they understood, could we still exchange for the small amount of money?" Xianggao took the paper and still wrapped it together with the documents in the bundle. He smiled and said to Chuntao, "Honey~"

Chuntao glanced at him and said, "I told you not to call me Honey."

Xianggao didn't respond to her and said, "What a coincidence that you got home early. Your business must be going well."

"I bought another basket in the morning, just like yesterday's."

"Haven't you said there are still a lot

left?"

"They all have been sent to the morning market and sold to the countryside for packing peanuts."

"It doesn't matter. Anyway, we made a good profit today. It's the first time that we have made thirty yuan. Since it's rare for both of us to be at home this afternoon, why not take a stroll in Shichahai to cool off?"

He entered the room and placed the bundle on the table. Chuntao also followed him inside. She said, "No, it won't do. We have guests today." As she spoke, she lifted the curtain and nodded to Xianggao, "You can go in."

Xianggao went in, and she followed. "This is my former husband." She told Xianggao, and then introduced him to Li Mao, "This is my current partner."

The two men faced each other, their four eyes meeting. If the distance between their eyeballs were equal, their gazes would connect in parallel. Neither of them said anything. Nor did the two flies resting on the windowsill. This caused the sunlight to be quietly moving for a minute or two.

"What's your surname?" Xianggao knew it, but had to ask as usual. They began to converse.

"I'm going to buy some food." Chuntao said to Xianggao again, "I think you haven't eaten food yet, have you? How about Chinese baked wheaten cakes?"

"I have already. You stay at home and I'll go buy it."

The woman pulled Xianggao onto the bed and said, "You stay here and talk to the guest." She gave him a smile before leaving.

Now there were two men left in the room. Under these circumstances, if they couldn't get along instantly, they would engage in a life-or-death battle. Fortunately, they chose the former. But we should never consider Li Mao incapable of fighting due to the loss of his two legs. We must remember Xianggao has spent three to five years writing and Li Mao can easily defeat him with strength. If he had a gun, it would be much easier. With just a flick of his finger, he could deal with Xiang Gao as easily as crossing a bridge.

Li Mao told Xianggao that Chuntao's father was a wealthy rural landlord with the ownership of an acre of land in the countryside. My father worked at his house and drove a donkey. Given that he was good at shooting, he married his daughter to him afraid that he would join the army in order for him to protect people in the village. These were never mentioned by Chuntao to him. He repeated what Chuntao had just said, gradually bringing their discussion to the personal issues concerning both of them.

"You two are reunited as a couple, so of

course I have to stay away." He said it reluctantly.

"No, I have left her for a long time, and I'm disabled now. I can't sustain her, so it's all in vain. You've lived together all these years. Why break apart? I can go to a home for the disabled. I've heard that there is a possibility to get in with personal connection."

This gave Xianggao a big surprise. He thought that although Li Mao was a soldier, he was never expected to have such chivalrous spirit. In spite of his willingness at heart, he had to express some reservations verbally. This was the subtlety of etiquette that educated people all understood.

"That doesn't make sense." Xiang Gao

said. "I don't want to be accused of taking someone else's wife. Think about it for your own sake. You wouldn't want your wife to live with someone else either."

"I can write her a divorce certificate, or write you a contract. Either way works." Li Mao said earnestly with a smile.

"Divorce? She did nothing wrong. You can't divorce her. I don't want to embarrass her. Sell her? I don't have the money to buy her. All my money belongs to her."

"I don't want any money."

"Then, what do you want?"

"I want nothing."

"Then why bother to write a sale contract?"

"Because words alone are not reliable and it would not be good if there were regrets later. Let's be cautious first, and noble later."

Just then, Chuntao returned with some Chinese baked wheaten cakes. Seeing the two having a great conversation, she felt quite pleased.

"I've been thinking lately that I need to find someone to help out. Bother Mao has come just in time. He can't move around, so it's just right for him to stay at home managing things and checking the paper. You can take charge of selling and I'll still be responsible for collecting. Let's start a business together as a trio." Chuntao proposed another idea.

Li Mao didn't refuse at all. He took a Chinese baked wheaten cake and stuffed it into his mouth as if he had just emerged from a world of starving ghosts, which left him no time to speak.

"Two men and one woman, starting a company? Is it funded by you?" Xianggao expressed unnecessary doubts.

"Don't you want to?" The woman asked.

"No, no, no, I don't mean anything." Xiang Gao had something to say but couldn't express it.

"What can I do? What can I accomplish, just sitting at home all day?" Li Mao was also a bit hesitant to support it. He understood what Xianggao was implying.

"You all don't need to worry. I have got an idea."

At this, Xianggao stuck out his tongue to lick his lips and swallowed a mouthful of saliva. Li Mao kept eating, but he gazed at Chuntao, waiting to hear her idea.

Collecting waste paper was probably a venture in the minds of females. In her mind, she had already decided that Li Mao should stay at home and sort out the old stamps and the pictures from cigarette boxes. This could be done as long as one had hands and eyes. She thought Li Mao's monthly food expenses would be covered if every day he could find a hundred or so cigarette pictures from the piles of waste paper. It wasn't bad to find two or three good and rare stamps every day. In this city, foreign cigarettes are sold at about ten thousand packs a day and it wasn't that difficult for her to collect one percent of the packs back. As for Xianggao, she still thought it better to have him look for celebrity letters or items that could be sold for more money. Needless to say, he had already been an expert and didn't need further guidance. She herself would do that laborious work and keep going out to collect goods regardless of strong winds and blazing sun except in heavy rain. She would work harder especially during bad weather, when some of her peers wouldn't go out.

She glanced at the sun through the window, realizing it was less than two o'clock. She stepped into the living room, put on her old straw hat, and leaned into the room to say to Xianggao, "I still need to find out if there are any items coming out of the palace. You stay at home and take care of him. We will discuss it again when I come back tonight." Xianggao couldn't stop her and let her go.

For several days, time passed quietly. However, it was certainly not ideal for two men and a woman to sleep together on the same bed. A society with polyandry couldn't become widespread after all. One reason was that most people had yet to free themselves from the primitive notions of marital authority and paternal authority.

This led to the customs and moral values. To be honest, in society, it was those who depended on and exploited people who tended to follow these so-called customs. As for those who lived by their own abilities, they didn't hold these in high regard. Take Chuntao for example. She was neither a madam nor a young lady. She wouldn't go to balls in diplomatic buildings, nor would she have the opportunity to be the center of attention at grand ceremonies. Her actions went uncriticized and unexamined. Even if there were criticisms, they didn't hurt her. It was only patrolmen who monitored her, but they were easy to cope with. As for the two men, Xianggao had the same values as Chuntao did except a few beliefs about social status which stemmed from little education he had received indeed and vague understanding of sage's teachings. But his life completely depended on Chuntao since they began living together. He had to listen to Chuntao's words which were like vitamins entering Chuntao's ears, for they were beneficial for him. Chuntao taught him not to be jealous, and he even uprooted the seeds of jealousy within him. As for Li Mao, he would stay if Chuntao and Xianggao were to let him stay. He would be satisfied if they were to acknowledge him as a relative. It was common for soldiers to give up one or two wives. But his difficulties were also concerned with social status. Although Xianggao did not feel jealous, various other insecurities frequently arose between the two men.

Even though the summer heat had not yet diminished, Chuntao and Xianggao were not the kind of people to go to Tangshan or Beidaihe for a holiday. During the day, they still had to go out to make a living. Staying at home, Li Mao had just begun to get the hang of this line of work. He could already distinguish which paper need be sent to Wanliutang or Tianning Temple for coarse paper, and which paper need be set aside, waiting for Xianggao's return for verification.

When Chuntao came back, it was Xianggao who attended to her as usual. It was already quite late. Smelling the odor of mosquito coils in the living room, she said to Xianggao who was sitting under the melon trellis, "We light mosquito coils so often. If we're not careful, no wonder we'll end up setting the house on fire."

Xianggao hadn't answered yet when Li Mao said, "That's not to drive away mosquitoes but to smoke out odors. I have Brother Liu light it. I'm going to sleep outside on the ground. It's really uncomfortable for us three to sleep together for it's too hot inside."

"Let me see whose red note is this on the table." Chuntao picked it up to take a look.

"We have made an agreement today that you belong to Brother Liu. That's a contract I made for him." The voice came from the bed in the room.

"Oh, you dare to discuss how to deal with me! But I cannot be assigned by you."

She took the red note into the room and

asked Li Mao, "Is this your idea or his?"

"It's ours. Otherwise, I will be upset. So will he."

"All in all, it's still the same point. Don't think of us as husband and wife, okay?"

She tore the red note into pieces, breathing heavily with anger.

"How much did you sell me for?"

"It's just writing down a few dozen yuan to make a good impression and giving away a wife for free. What a failure!"

"Does selling a wife mean success?" She came out and said to Xianggao, "Now that you have money, you can buy a wife, huh? If you had a little more money—"

"Don't say that. Don't say that." Xianggao interrupted her, "Chuntao, you don't understand. These past few days, my peers have been mocking me."

"What are they mocking you about?"

"They're mocking me—" Xianggao couldn't find the words. In fact, he didn't have much prejudice. Whatever Chuntao wanted to do, he went along with her nine times out of ten. He himself didn't understand what this power was. Behind her, if he thought things should be done, they should go as he wished.

However, once he saw her, he felt as if

he were facing the Empress Dowager Cixi, having to obey her every decree.

"Oh, you have been studying for a couple of days after all. You're afraid of being criticized and laughed at."

Since ancient times, what actually rules the public hasn't been the teachings of sages but seemingly the whips that strike and the tongues that scold. Customs and manners are maintained through punishment and reprimand. However, in Chuntao's mind, she held an attitude of "if others strike, I'll strike; if others scold, I'll scold". She was not weak. She didn't strike or scold others, nor would she allow herself to be struck or scolded. We can tell this from the way she admonished Xianggao.

"If someone laughs at you, won't you hit him? Why did you show fear? Our business is no one else's concern."

Xianggao had nothing to say.

"Let's not mention this again. Why don't we three keep living like this?"

The whole room fell silent. After supper, Xianggao and Chuntao were still sitting under the melon trellis, but they didn't chat as much as they used to.

Li Mao called Chuntao into the room, urging her to return to Xianggao's side. He said that she didn't understand a man's thought that no one wanted to be a turtle, an insult implying being an unfaithful or dishonorable person and taking another man's wife wasn't well-reputed. He took out a red letter that had turned dark brown from his waist and handed it to Chuntao, saying, "This is our wedding letter. When I escaped that night, I took it from the altar and tucked it into my bosom. Now you can take it away so that we aren't counted as a couple any longer."

Chuntao took the red letter without saying a word, her eyes fixed on the tattered mat on the bed. She couldn't help sitting down next to the disabled man and said, "Brother Mao, I cannot accept this. Please take it back. I'm still your wife. A night of marriage brings a hundred days of affection. I won't do anything immoral. If I were to reject you when seeing you unable to move today and unable to perform any heavy work, could I still consider myself a decent person?"

She placed the red letter on the bed.

Li Mao was deeply moved at her words. He said to Chuntao softly, "I can see you really love him. It's better for you to be with him. When you have some money, you can either send me back to the countryside or to a home for the disabled."

"To be honest with you," Chuntao's voice lowered, "I have been living with him for the past few years just like a couple and everything has gone smoothly as I wish. I feel really reluctant to part with him. Why not call him in to discuss it and see what ideas he has?" She called out towards the window, "Brother Xiang! Brother Xiang!" But there was no response at all. When she went out to take a look, Brother Xiang was already gone.

This was his first time going out in the evening. She paused for a moment and then addressed the man in the room, "I'll go look for him".

She posited that Xianggao wouldn't go anywhere else. When she reached the end of the alley, she asked Mr. Wu. Mr. Wu said he went over to that side of the main street. She went to the usual place where he did business, but didn't find him there. It's easy for people to get lost. If you can't see them, they seem to drift away into a vast, unsearchable place. Not until almost one o'clock did she finally return home in frustration.

The oil lamp in the room had already gone out.

"Have you fallen asleep? Has Brother Xiang come back?" She went into the room, took out a match and lit the lamp. She glanced at the bed and saw Li Mao hanging himself from the window sill with his own belt. Although her heart was inevitably filled with fear as a woman, she still had courage to climb up and loosen him. Fortunately, it didn't take long for her to gradually wake him up by gently rubbing him with no need to bother anyone else.

It embodies a heroic spirit to kill oneself for others' sake. If Li Mao still had his two legs, he wouldn't have had to resort to such measures. In the past two or three days, he always felt that he had little hope and it would be better to end his life so that Chuntao could live well. Although Chuntao had no love for him, she had a strong sense of loyalty. She comforted him with many words until dawn. He fell asleep and Chuntao got off the bed. Seeing some ashes on the ground and some unburned red letter left, she recognized it as the wedding letter that Li Mao had given her and stared blankly at it.

She didn't go out that day and sat on the bed with Li Mao until evening.

"What are you crying for?" Chuntao asked him when she saw Li Mao's hot tears rolling down.

"I'm sorry for what I've done to you.

What am I here for?"

"No one blames you for coming."

"He has left now and I've lost my two legs."

"Don't think like that. I believe he will come back."

"I hope that he will come back."

Another day passed. Chuntao got up, went to the melon shed to pick two cucumbers for cooking, quickly baked a large Chinese flatbread, and brought it into the room for both of them to share.

She still wore the worn-out hat and

carried a basket on her back.

"Don't go out since you don't seem very happy today!" Li Mao said to her through the window.

"It makes me feel even more restless to stay at home."

She paced slowly out of the door. Working was her nature. Even in a gloomy state of mind, she still felt the need to be productive. Chinese women seem to focus only on life rather than on love. What she was concerned with was the development of life while the development of love stirred only in a dull and gloomy state of mind. Naturally, love is merely a feeling, whereas life is substantial. The Kamasutra discussed while spending all day lying in luxurious tents or sitting in secluded woods is knowledge that comes from the Queen's Ship or the President's Ship. Chuntao was neither a sister of the tide-riders nor a student of the blue-eyed foreigners. She couldn't understand it and could only be left puzzled.

She passed one alley after another. Boundless dust and endless roads surged with this heavy-hearted woman. Sometimes she shouted, "I'll exchange waste paper for foreign lamps and sometimes she didn't even pick up a pile of old newspapers by the roadside that didn't need exchanging. Sometimes when she should give two boxes of lamps, she instead gave five ones. After getting through a day in a disorganized way, she slowly walked home along with those in black who only shouted and scrambled for food. She looked up at the newly posted household registration document which listed the household head as Mrs. Liu, the household head and felt even more distressed.

Just as she stepped into the courtyard, Xianggao rushed out from the house.

She stared with wide eyes and only said, "You came back—" while the rest of what she wanted to say came out in tears.

"I can't leave you. Everything I've achieved is ascribed to you. I know you need my help. I cannot be heartless and ungrateful." In fact, he had been wandering aimlessly on the street for the past couple of days, having no idea where to go. When he walked, he felt as if heavy iron shackles were fastened to his feet, the other end tethered to Chuntao's hand. Moreover, he encountered everywhere the advertisements stating "He's still the best", which constantly stirred his mood to the point that he didn't even realize he was hungry.

"I have already settled it with Brother Xiang. He's the household's head and I'm his roommate."

Xianggao helped her take off the basket as usual and meanwhile wiped away the tears from her face. He said, "If we go back to the countryside, he'll be the household's head, I'll be the roommate, and you will be our wife."

Not saying a word, she went straight into the house, took off her clothes and hat, and carried out her daily cleansing.

The business was being discussed under the melon trellis once again. They were considering that after selling out the batch of waste paper with written characters from the palace Xianggao could set up a small stall in the market or move into a slightly larger house.

Inside the house, the tiny light, as small as a bean, was extinguished by a gourd lantern that flew in from the melon trellis. Li Miao had long fallen into a deep sleep, as the Milky Way hung low in the sky.

"Let's go to sleep as well." The woman said.

"You lie down first. I'll massage your legs for you in a little while."

"There's no need for that since I didn't walk much today. Get up early tomorrow and remember to handle that batch of business. We haven't opened business for several days."

"I forgot to bring it to you earlier. When I got home today and saw you weren't back yet, I specifically went to the overpass to bring back a 80% brand-new hat for you. Take a look!" He fumbled for the hat in the dark, ready to hand it to her.

"I can't see it right now! I'll wear it tomorrow instead."

The courtyard was silent, with only the fragrance of evening primrose lingering in the air. From inside the house, one could faintly hear the dialogues like "Honey" and "I don't like that. I'm not your wife."

www.ingramcontent.com/pod-product-compliance
Lightning Source LLC
Chambersburg PA
CBHW070426310726
48977CB00003B/859